Gargoylz

Magic at the Museum

Gargoylz: grotesque stone creatures found on old buildings, spouting rainwater from the guttering. Sometimes seen causing mischief and mayhem before scampering away over rooftops.

Read all the
Gargoylz adventures!

Gargoylz

Magic at the Museum

Burchett & Vogler

illustrated by Leighton Noyes

RED FOX

GARGOYLZ: MAGIC AT THE MUSEUM
A RED FOX BOOK 978 1 849 41078 6

First published in Great Britain by Red Fox,
an imprint of Random House Children's Books
A Random House Group Company

This edition published 2010

1 3 5 7 9 10 8 6 4 2

Series created and developed by Amber Caravéo
Copyright © Random House Children's Books, 2010

The Random House Group Limited supports the Forest Stewardship Council
(FSC), the leading international forest certification organization. All our titles
that are printed on Greenpeace-approved FSC-certified paper carry the FSC
logo. Our paper procurement policy can be found at
www.rbooks.co.uk/environment

Set in Bembo Schoolbook

Red Fox Books are published by Random House Children's Books,
61–63 Uxbridge Road, London W5 5SA

www.**kids**at**randomhouse**.co.uk
www.**rbooks**.co.uk

Addresses for companies within The Random House Group Limited can be
found at: www.randomhouse.co.uk/offices.htm

THE RANDOM HOUSE GROUP L... ... ...

A CIP catalogue record for this book is available from the British Library.

Printed and bound in Great Britain by CPI Bookmarque, Croydon, CR0 4TD

For Jennifer Burchett, whose visits to the Natural
History Museum are forever etched in our memories
- Burchett & Vogler

For Jackie Clark and Pete Gowers who opened the door
and illuminated the path
- Leighton Noyes

Hello, I'm the Web Gargoyle.
Look out for me – I'll be hiding in one
of the pictures in the book.
When you spot me, be sure to make a
note of the secret codeword I'm holding.
The codeword unlocks a secret level
of the amazing Gargoylz game
on our fabulous website at
www.gargoylz.co.uk

Oldacre Primary School

St Mark's Church

playground

badger checking if the coast is clear

School Report - Max Black

Days absent: 0

Days late: 0

Max is never afraid to make a contribution to history lessons. His demonstration of a battering ram using a broom and a bucket was very realistic, although the resulting hole in the classroom door was not ideal.

I worry that Max only seems to play with Ben Neal, but he assures me he has a lot of friends at the local church.

Class teacher - Miss Deirdre Bleet

Max Black's behaviour this term has been outrageous. He has repeatedly broken school rule number 739: boys must not tell 'knock knock' jokes in assembly. He is still playing pranks with Ben Neal. Mrs Pumpkin is absent again after the exploding paint pot incident. And Mrs Simmer, the head dinner lady, says the mincing machine has never been the same since he fed his maths test into it.

Head teacher - Hagatha Hogsbottom (Mrs)

School Report - Ben Neal

Days absent: 0

Days late: 0

This term Ben has been very inventive in PE. However, attempting to tightrope-walk across the hall was a little dangerous - and used up all the skipping ropes. He spends far too much time in class looking out of the window and waving at the gravestones in the churchyard. He would be better learning his spellings - a word he insists on writing as 'spellingz'.

Class teacher - Miss Deirdre Bleet

Ben Neal is always polite, but I am deeply concerned about his rucksack. It often looks very full - and not with school books, I am certain. It has sometimes been seen to wriggle and squirm. I suspect that he is keeping a pet in there. If so, it is outrageous and there will be trouble.

Head teacher - Hagatha Hogsbottom (Mrs)

Contents

1. Rocket Ride

Max Black and Ben Neal zoomed up
to Oldacre Primary School on their
imaginary spy jet-scooters. They wore
rucksacks on their backs and were pulling
wheelie suitcases behind them. The clock
on the church next to the school was just
striking six in the morning.

"Here come the world's top superspies
on their dawn mission," yelled Max,
screeching in at the gates. "All set for a
school trip to the Museum of Space and
Time in London."

"We're the first ones to arrive, Agent

Black!" exclaimed Ben.

"You know what that means, Agent Neal," said Max with a grin. "Gargoyle time!"

Max and Ben had some unusual friends. They were gargoylz, the little stone statues that hung on the old church. The boys were the only humans who knew the gargoylz could come to life and that each one had a special power. Their favourite thing in the world was playing tricks – which suited Max and Ben perfectly.

Max and Ben whizzed into the churchyard and flung down their cases.

"Strange," said Max. "There's not a gargoyle in sight. I wonder where they are."

All at once there was a loud rumbling snore from the roof of the vicar's house next door. There, curled up in a heap by the chimney, lay Toby, Azzan, Zack and Bart. The boys grinned at each other.

"I'm sure they wouldn't want to be asleep when we're awake, Agent Black," said Ben mischievously.

"Time for a trick, Agent Neal," declared Max.

3

The boys tiptoed up to the vicar's garden wall.

"One . . . two . . . three . . ." whispered Ben.

"GREETINGZ!" the boys yelled.

The pile of gargoylz shot into the air. Zack vanished with a **pop**, Toby flew into a tree and Azzan was so surprised that he let out a blast of flame from his dragony snout, scorching Bart on the bottom. Azzan's special power often got him into trouble.

"It's only us," shouted Max, waving over the wall at them.

Pop! Zack reappeared and the gargoylz beamed at the boys. All except Bart – but he was often grumpy. The chubby little gargoyle flapped at his singed gladiator skirt and grumbled under his breath as he scrambled down to join Max and Ben.

"Dangling drainpipes!" said Toby in his growly purr as he looped the loop over their heads. "That was a good prank, boyz."

"I was very nearly a bonfire!" complained Bart.

"It was only a tiny flame," said Azzan cheerfully.

"It's really early," said Toby, giving a huge yawn.

"How come you're at school?"

"Couldn't sleep?" suggested Zack.

Max laughed. "We had to be here early," he told them. "Our class is going on a school trip—"

"—to a museum full of dinosaurs and spaceships!" Ben burst in.

"And the best bit is," added Max in a rush, "we're going to have a sleepover there – tonight!"

"Can we come?" asked Toby, his monkey face full of excitement.

"That's a brilliant idea!" exclaimed Max.

"I like school trips! I like school trips!"

shouted Zack, shaking his mane in delight.

Max and Ben could hear chattering from the playground now. Everyone else was arriving. It was nearly time to go.

"But how can the gargoylz come without being seen?" asked Ben, scratching his head.

"Easy," declared Max. "We can put them in our cases. My mum's packed loads of stuff I don't need – I bet yours has too!"

Ben grinned. "Secret Plan: Pack the Gargoylz."

"We'd better be quick," said Max. He could see his classmates lining up, ready to walk to the station.

The boys grabbed the handles of their wheelie cases and raced off through the playground and into the school.

In two minutes flat they had stuffed their toothbrushes, pyjamas, towels and other useless items under their desks and returned to the churchyard. Max unzipped his case, which now contained a comic, a rolled-up sleeping bag and an odd sock.

Toby immediately jumped in. Azzan bounced in next to him.

"Don't need to hide," insisted Zack. "I'll just disappear."

"It won't work. You know you'll get too excited and end up popping into view," said Ben.

Zack could make himself completely invisible to all humans but he wasn't very good at staying that way.

He ran three times round the church and dived headfirst into Ben's empty case.

"Coming, Bart?" asked Ben.

"Might as well," said the little gargoyle grumpily, "though I don't like museums." He squeezed in beside Zack. "There's not much room," they heard him complain as they zipped up the cases.

Suddenly they heard a booming voice bellowing from the playground. Max's spy radar whirred into action: grey hair, beaky nose, guaranteed to scare the scariest of witches. He knew what that meant. It was Enemy Agent Mrs Hogsbottom, commonly known as Mrs Hogsbum, codename: Evil Head Teacher.

"Outrageous!" she thundered over the wall. "Max Black and Ben Neal, you have broken school rule number five hundred and twenty-two – boys must not loiter in the churchyard when they are going on a school trip to London."

The boys dutifully dragged their cases into the playground and took their places in the line.

"If only Mrs Hogsbum knew who was coming with us!" whispered Max.

"She'd probably explode," replied Ben with a grin.

Their teacher, Miss Bleet, was standing at the front of the line with the other teachers accompanying the class trip, Mr Widget and Mrs Stearn. "Off we go," she called out nervously.

They set off down the road to the railway station.

"Make sure you behave yourselves!" they heard Mrs Hogsbottom yell from the playground. "And don't you dare get lost on the Underground. School rule number one hundred and . . ." Her voice faded as the class went round the corner.

Later that day Max and Ben's class marched up the steps of the Museum of Space and Time and burst through the swing doors.

"Look at that T. rex!" gasped Ben, gawping at the huge skeleton that seemed to fill the whole entrance hall. "It's awesome."

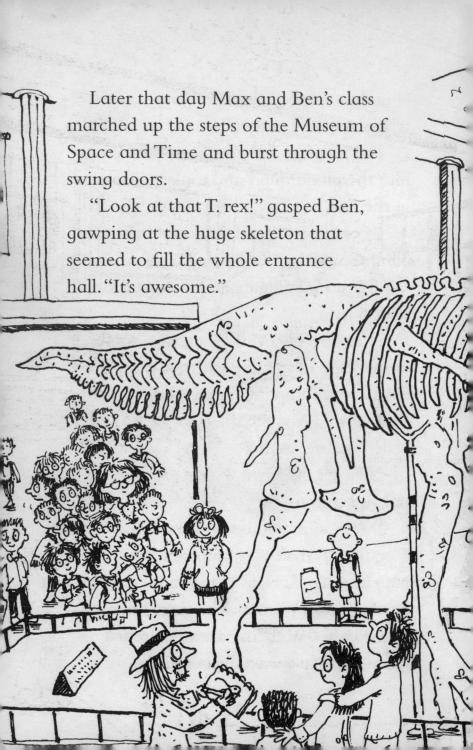

"And the sign over there says **Space Zone**!" gabbled Max excitedly. "This is going to be so cool." A smiling woman with dark hair came over. "Welcome to the museum sleepover experience!" she said brightly.

"I'm Alison – your guide during your stay.
Let's put your cases in our storeroom."

"I want to get out!" came Toby's
growly purr.

Alison looked at Max, puzzled.

"I mean," said Max hurriedly, giving
his case a nudge, "I want to get *into* the
museum."

"You won't have to wait long!" said
their guide. "Follow me."

"We can't leave the gargoylz in our
cases all day," Ben whispered anxiously to
Max. "They'll miss all the fun."

"If we make sure we're last in the storeroom," Max whispered back, "we can let them out when everyone else has gone."

After the rest of the class had run back to the entrance hall, Max and Ben dragged their cases through the storeroom door. The room was small and cramped, stuffed with old furniture and labelled crates. The boys opened their suitcases and Toby, Zack and Azzan burst out. Their faces fell as they stared at the pile of bags.

"Is this it?" asked Zack.

"These aren't very exciting exhibits," said Toby.

Azzan gave a puff of smoke as he sniffed around the cases. "They don't look much like dinosaurs," he complained.

"I told you it wasn't worth coming," said Bart grumpily, poking his head out.

Max and Ben burst out laughing.

"These aren't the exhibits," said Max. "We'll see all the fun stuff in a minute."

"Hop in and you can come with us," said Ben, holding his rucksack open.

Toby dived into Max's bag and Azzan climbed into Ben's.

"Oh dear," said Max. "There's no room for Bart and Zack."

"I'm staying here," said Bart firmly. He zipped himself back into Ben's case, and in a muffled voice added, "I need to catch up on my sleep . . ." Soon loud snores could be heard.

"And I'll just stay invisible," declared

Zack, doing a triple somersault and disappearing with a **pop**.

"Well, make sure you do," warned Max as he opened the door.

Alison was handing out name badges, clipboards and museum maps. "These are for your work," she told the children.

"I hate work!" came Toby's growly voice from Max's rucksack.

"Pardon?" said Alison.

"Er . . ." burbled Max. "I said, 'Great work!'"

"It's nice to see you're so keen," said Alison. "Follow me, everyone."

"I wonder where we're going," said Ben.

"Hope it's the Space section," said Max, eagerly checking his map.

"Or the Earthquake Zone!" added Ben.

"Dinosaurs!" Azzan's muffled voice could be heard from Ben's rucksack.

"Monsters of the deep!" called an invisible Zack from somewhere up a pillar.

But Alison led them into a dull-looking room with display cabinets full of pots that had peculiar bushes growing in them.

"Plants," whispered Max in disgust. "What a waste of time. There are enough of them in my garden at home."

He and Ben stood at the

back of the group while Alison pointed out unusual leaf formations and said long words like "respiration" and "chlorophyll", which the boys didn't understand.

Ben suddenly felt a surge of heat on his back and got a faint whiff of burning plastic. "Can I get out now?" hissed Azzan.

"No," Ben hissed back. "Everyone will see you. And stop melting my rucksack."

Max began to wriggle.

21

"What's up?" Ben whispered. "You look as if you've got ants in your pants."

"It's Toby," said Max, fidgeting. "He's fed up. He keeps poking me."

At that moment they caught the flash of a dragony tail in the leaves of a banana tree in the corner. It quickly disappeared, but the next instant the whole of Zack could be seen waving cheerily at them from a vine on the ceiling.

"He's forgetting to stay invisible," groaned Ben.

"Emergency, Agent Neal," said Max in a low voice. "We must use our super secret sneaking powers to get the gargoylz away from here before they're discovered."

"And now's our chance, Agent Black!" exclaimed Ben as Alison led the class round a corner towards "Moulds of the World". When everyone was out of sight, the boys ran out into the corridor and dived through the nearest door.

They found themselves in a dimly lit, mysterious-looking room. No one was around. Toby and Azzan scrambled out of the rucksacks.

"About time!" exclaimed Toby. "We've been in there for hourz."

"Dayz probably," said Azzan.

"It's only been ten minutes," Max told them.

Azzan was looking around the room.

"No dinosaurs here either."

Pop! Zack appeared in front of them. "Who put the lights out?" he asked, scratching his head.

"It's dark because we're in the Space Zone," explained Ben, squinting at his map. "And it's awesome!"

All around the dark room hung glowing models of the planets,

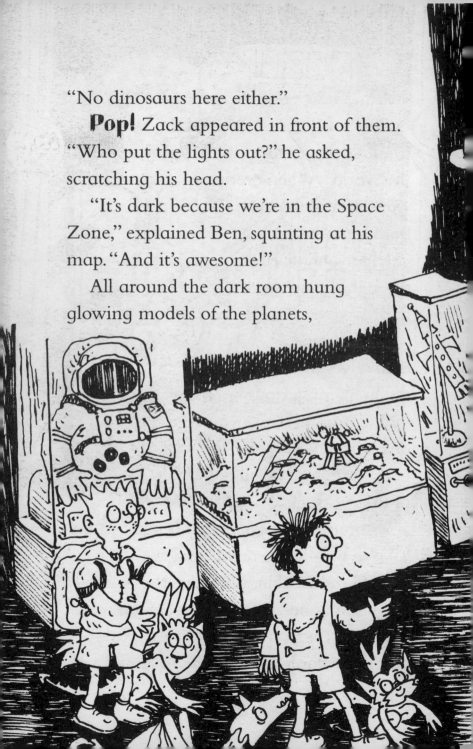

orbiting a giant sun.
And at the far end was a
gigantic silver rocket. Its pointed
nose almost touched the ceiling.
A TRIP TO THE MOON! said the words over
the rocket door.

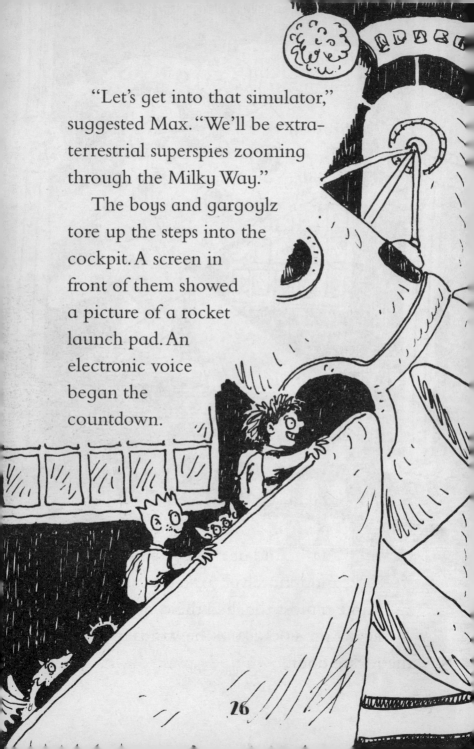

"Let's get into that simulator," suggested Max. "We'll be extra-terrestrial superspies zooming through the Milky Way."

The boys and gargoylz tore up the steps into the cockpit. A screen in front of them showed a picture of a rocket launch pad. An electronic voice began the countdown.

"**Ten . . . nine . . . eight . . .**"

"Funny way to count," said Azzan.

"**Seven . . . six . . . five . . . four . . .**"

"They always count backwards when a rocket's about to take off," said Ben, strapping himself into a seat. "Hold on tight."

"**Three . . . two . . . one . . . BLAST OFF!**"

There was a deafening roar and the cockpit began to shake violently.

"We're on our way to the moon!" cried Max in excitement.

"It feels like my tummy's on the ceiling!" laughed Ben.

The gargoylz were tumbling around the cockpit, squealing with delight as the ride moved up and down and upside down.

Zack ran up and down the walls and
Azzan blew excited flames and puffs of
smoke into the air.

"Spluttering gutterz!" exclaimed Toby.
"I've never flown like this before."

The simulator jerked and rocked and
spun.

"We're in outer space now!" gasped
Ben, pointing at the stars flashing past on
the screen.

"And we're upside down!" yelled Max as his hair stood on end. "Awesome!"

"**Prepare for touchdown!**" came the electronic voice.

There was a tremendous shaking and a loud thump, and everything was still. The screen showed the moon's surface outside the window. Then the rocket took off and zoomed back to Earth, shaking and tumbling its delighted passengers around again. Finally the cockpit righted itself and the doors to the simulator slid open.

"Fantastic!" exclaimed Max.

"Flame-tastic!" yelled Azzan.

"Shame Bart missed it," said Ben.

Toby grinned. "I haven't had so much fun since Zack jumped on the end of a loose floorboard and catapulted the vicar into the sink."

They clambered dizzily out of the simulator. Toby and Azzan had just scrambled back inside the rucksacks when they heard a voice.

"Max and Ben! What are you doing in here?"

Pop! Zack disappeared. Max's spy radar came to life: small, twitchy, and a nose for smelling trouble at a hundred paces. Max knew what that meant. It was Enemy Agent Mrs Stearn, codename: Strict Supply Teacher. She was standing at the entrance of the Space Zone, glaring at them.

SPY FILE:

Codename: Strict Supply Teacher

"I've been looking for you two," she
snapped. "You should be in the biology
section with everyone else."

"We were doing biology research," said
Ben, trying to stand upright.

Mrs Stearn looked at the rocket
simulator. "What kind of research?" she
demanded.

Max dizzily tried to bring the teacher
into focus. "The effect of space travel on
the human body," he said in a rush. "Did
you know that you get wobbly legs when
you've been to the moon?"

"No I didn't," said Mrs Stearn, frowning. "And your tummy goes up to the ceiling," added Ben.

"It's great!" finished Max.

"That doesn't sound like research to me," sniffed Mrs Stearn. "You're not to go on the simulator again."

Max and Ben gazed at each other in disappointment. They'd been looking forward to having another go.

Just then the rest of the class came in, gasping with delight at the sight of the Space Zone. Mrs Stearn went over to supervise.

"Everyone line up for the space ride," called Mr Widget. "Get in line, Max and Ben."

"Better do what the teacher says!" said Max, exchanging grins with Ben as they ran to join the queue.

2. Where's Bart?

Max and Ben stood in the museum foyer, watching the last visitors walk past the T. rex and out through the doors.

"Look at those poor people having to leave because it's closing time," said Max pityingly.

"Not us, Agent Black," said Ben. "We're about to have an amazing sleepover."

"Us too," called Toby from Max's rucksack.

"We haven't forgotten about you," Max assured him. "Keep hidden a bit longer and then you can share our sleeping bags.

We'll fetch Bart too."

The boys had had a great time. They'd rattled about in the Earthquake Zone, run through the Black Hole Experience and watched a velociraptor eat a protoceratops. Then they'd had a slap-up tea of Stone-age Nuggets and Triassic Chips in the café, while their gargoyle friends sat in a bin, happily munching a half-eaten packet of chocolate chip cookies.

"Gather round, everyone," called Alison when they'd finished eating. "It's time for me to show you where you'll be spending the night."

Max and Ben promised the gargoylz they'd come back for them later and then followed Alison to a large room with a deep carpet. In one corner was a pile of pillows, and right in the middle, on a wooden platform, stood the fearsome skeleton of a sabre-toothed tiger, long fangs gleaming.

A dreadful shriek pierced Max's ears. He activated his spy radar: clean uniforms, pink ribbons, flowery hairslides. He knew what that meant. It was three Enemy Agents: Lucinda Tellingly, Poppy Parker and Tiffany Goodchild.

"Great!" Max whispered to Ben. "The girls are frightened of the skeleton!"

But to their surprise, Lucinda was pointing at *them*. "We've got to sleep in the same room as those stinky boys," she complained.

"Gross!" chorused Poppy and Tiffany, turning their noses up as they flounced past.

"They're not getting away with that!" said Ben.

"No chance, Agent Neal," muttered Max. "I've got a great idea for a trick. Secret Plan: Frighten the Girls. And Mr Sabre-tooth over there will give us a helping paw."

They sauntered over to Lucinda and her chums.

"You're ever so brave sleeping in the same room as the skeleton," Max told them. "Especially after what happened to the last school party. They completely disappeared."

"The sabre-toothed
skeleton came to life, you
see," said Ben.

"And it gobbled them
all up," added Max with a
shudder, "teachers and all."

"They only found three
socks and a mangled clipboard,"
Ben went on mysteriously.

"That's ridiculous!" snorted
Lucinda. "It's just a pile of old
bones. Come on, girls. We'll show
them we're not scared."

And to Max and Ben's amazement
they each grabbed a pillow and settled
themselves down right under the nose of
the sabre-tooth.

"Everyone to the storeroom to get your
night things!" called Mr Widget.

"I'm really disappointed, Agent Neal,"
said Max as they mooched along behind
the others. "Girls are usually a lot wimpier
than that."

"We'll think of another trick to play
on them later," said Ben. "Let's make sure
we're last in the storeroom. Then we can
get Bart for the sleepover."

Max and Ben waited for everyone else
to go. Ben was just bending down to let
Bart out of his case when a sharp voice
interrupted him.

"Hurry up, boys," Mrs Stearn said,
bustling in. "You only need your
sleeping bags, pyjamas
and toothbrushes."

Before they
could stop
her, she'd
flung Ben's
case open.
"What's the
meaning of this?"
she demanded,
turning to face him.

Max and Ben looked at each other in horror. She must have found Bart! They had to make an excuse.

"That's my, er . . . lucky teddy," said Ben.

"He always takes it on sleepovers," added Max hurriedly.

"What are you babbling about?" asked Mrs Stearn. "There's no teddy in here. And no nightclothes either!"

Ben peered into the case. Bart was nowhere to be seen. Ben looked at Max. What had happened to their grumpy little gargoyle friend? Unfortunately, they couldn't look for him now. Mrs Stearn was tapping her foot impatiently.

"Where are all your things?" she insisted.

"I don't know," said Ben. "They've vanished!"

"Along with his teddy," muttered Max.

Ben put on his special wide-eyed, innocent face. It always worked on the dinner ladies, who gave him extra apple crumble. It didn't work on the supply teacher.

"Pyjamas don't just vanish," she said.

Max flung open his case. "Mine have gone as well!" he gasped in mock surprise.

"I might have known you two would cause trouble," sighed Mrs Stearn. "Well, you'll just have to sleep in your clothes.

Now come and join the others."

Max and Ben followed her back to the
sleepover room.

"I wonder where Bart's got to,"
whispered Max as they laid out their
sleeping bags.

"We must look for him," said Ben. "He
could have wandered off and got lost.
After all, the museum's huge!"

"We'll wait until everyone's asleep,"
said Max. "Then we'll collect the other
gargoylz from the café bin and start
searching."

* * *

Soon everyone was asleep — except for Max and Ben.

"Listen to those snores!" hissed Max.

"Lucinda's the loudest!" Ben whispered back. "She sounds like a warthog with a cold!"

"I reckon it's safe for us to go now," said Max.

They crept down the long dark corridors to the café. Following munching sounds, they found Toby, Azzan and Zack under a table scoffing a pile of sausage rolls.

"Bart's missing!" Ben told them.

"That's terrible!" Azzan exclaimed, roasting his snack with a worried blast of flame.

"We must find him," said Toby.

"Off we go! Off we go!" said Zack, stuffing three sausage rolls into his mouth and jumping up.

"Let's try the animal exhibits first," suggested Max. "They're the nearest to the storeroom."

"I'll scout ahead," said Toby. He flew off and they quickly followed him down the corridor and into a large hall full of stuffed animals.

Moonlight from the windows cast deep shadows across the room. The first display featured huge grizzly bears. Their mouths were open in fierce snarls and their glassy eyes seemed to follow the boys as they tiptoed past.

"This place is a bit creepy at night," said Ben.

Azzan snorted a puff of smoke. "I'll protect you," he said bravely.

"Fight the bears!" exclaimed Zack, rushing up to the biggest one and bumping his nose on the glass. "Ouch! He hit me."

"No he didn't," said Max. "They're not alive."

"That one was," huffed Zack, rubbing his snout.

They walked on past lions, tigers and cheetahs, all in stalking poses.

"Welcome to Bat World!" bellowed a voice ahead, making them all jump. "Bats are nocturnal so they come out when you are sleeping."

"We've triggered some sort of interactive exhibit," said Max, gazing in admiration as lights flashed on and a flock of model bats fluttered over their heads.

"Cool animatronics!" said Ben. "They look alive."

"Spluttering gutterz!" cried Toby.
"Bart's in there! I can see the tip of his
wing. He's upside down on the ceiling."

"That's not him," laughed Ben. "That's
a fruit bat."

Toby peered hard at the wing. "You're
right," he said. "It's not ugly enough to be
Bart."

They slipped quietly on past the bats
and into the next room, where they
stopped by a family of stuffed meerkats.

"This museum's huge," said Max. "We'll

never be able to search it all in one night."

"We need to think like Bart," said Zack.

"That's a good idea!" exclaimed Ben. "If we can think like a grumpy gargoyle we might work out where he's gone."

Zack was so pleased with himself he **popped** in and out of view.

"How do we think like Bart?" asked Azzan. "No one's as grumpy as him."

Max pulled his mouth down. "I'm grumpy now," he said.

"I'll tell a corny joke like Bart does," volunteered Ben. "What kind of horses come out at night?"

"I don't know," said Toby.

"What kind of horsez come out at night?"

"Night-mares!"

"I've got one," said Azzan when they'd
finished laughing. "Where do cowz
go to see statues?" He squirmed with
excitement, sending out small jets of fire.
"To a *moo*-seum!"

"Good one," said Max. "But it's not
helping us find Bart."

"Spiderz!" yelled Zack, pointing
across the floor. "Spiderz!"

A trail of assorted spiders
was marching towards
them. As they watched,
the ones at the front
faded away.

"Bart burped
those with his special
power!" cried Max,
jumping to his feet.
"If we find out where
they've come from,
we'll find him."

The spiders were scuttling out from the next room. Carefully avoiding the little creatures, the boys and gargoylz followed the trail, and stepped into the Dino Zone. Huge dinosaur shapes loomed out of the darkness.

"That T. rex skeleton looks super-
scary," whispered Ben. "It's incredible!"
"Something's moving!" gasped Toby,
pointing to the far corner of the room.

"Good prank, Toby," said Max with a grin. "But you can't fool me. These bags of bones have been dead for millions of years."

"I'm not joking!" insisted Toby. "Look!"

The boys looked. Toby was right. There was a flurry of wings and claws in the shadowy corner, and then suddenly a dark shape came scratching and scuttling straight towards them. It was as big as Toby and had a long sharp beak, glittering eyes and flapping wings.

"It's a pterodactyl!" Max's voice came out in a squeak. "And it's coming straight for us!"

"I'll save you!" yelled Azzan, jumping bravely in front of the boys. He took in a deep breath and let out a burst of yellow flame. Caught in the stream of fire, the pterodactyl melted before their eyes until all that was left was a gleaming puddle of gloopy purple goo.

"What have you done?" came a familiar grumpy voice.

"It's Bart!" shouted Toby in delight.

The frowning gargoyle stomped out from behind a stegosaurus. He had a look of horror on his face. "You've melted my new friend!"

"What do you mean?" asked Max, peering down at the goo.

"He lives here in the museum," said Bart. "At least he *did*." He pulled anxiously at his gladiator skirt. "I met him in the storeroom and we got on really well. Now he's been liquefied."

"Sorry," said Azzan, giving the goo a poke with his paw. "I didn't know he was your friend."

"Something's happening," said Ben suddenly.

Ripples were running across the puddle of goo. It began to bubble and gurgle. Everyone jumped back.

"I'm not melted for ever!" said a chirpy voice, and the purple liquid bulged up until the little pterodactyl was standing in front of them again. His winged arms and short legs ended in long claws and, like the gargoylz, his skin was stone-coloured. "I was just using my special power," he told them, his eyes dancing with fun.

Bart gave him a hug. "I'm so glad you're all right," he cried. "This is Toby, Azzan and Zack – I live with them on our church. They're gargoylz like you and me. And these two are Max and Ben."

"They're humanz!" exclaimed the little pterodactyl. "We mustn't be seen by

humanz. Quick, chaps, hide!" He quivered
and began to melt again.

"No need," Bart told him quickly.
"These are special humanz. They're our
friendz."

The little gargoyle solidified again.
"Oh, good show!" he said. He held out
a wing. There was a chunk missing from
one point. "Jolly pleased to meet you. My
name's Jehieli."

"It's pronounced Je-hee-ay-lee," said
Bart importantly.

"Jehelly . . . ?" said Toby.

"Jeeheeby . . . ?" tried Azzan.

"Jayjee laylee . . . ?" Max frowned. "It's
a bit hard to say."

Jehieli's beak turned down.

"But it's an awesome name," Ben said quickly. "And what makes it really cool is that it sounds a bit like your secret power – turning to *jelly*."

The pterodactyl perked up. "That's the ticket," he said. "You can call me Jelly. I was delighted to meet Bart in the storeroom. I'd been in there for ages."

"He speaks like someone from those old black and white filmz I watch at your house," Toby whispered to Max.

"Jelly used to live on a church," explained Bart. "But it got bombed in the Second World War."

"Is that how your wing got chipped?"

57

asked Ben. "Is it a war wound?"

Jelly nodded proudly. "The museum was supposed to repair me. But they never got round to it. I've been in the storeroom ever since I got rescued from the ruinz. It's jolly to meet some new friendz."

"Jolly Jelly!" burst out Zack, running around in excited circles. "Jolly Jelly!" He collided with a glass case full of teeth and rebounded into the triceratops. The huge skeleton wobbled, its bones rattling together spookily.

"It looks as if it's alive," said Ben in delight.

"Hey! That's given me an idea, Agent Neal," said Max. "Time for a new Secret Plan: Frighten the Girls. And this time it's going to work. They didn't believe us when we said the sabre-toothed tiger could move. Well, they'll believe it in a minute. We're going to play an awesome trick and we need your special power, Zack."

"Whizzo!" declared Jelly. "I've only just met you and we're off to play a prank already!"

Max explained his plan to the gargoylz and they all crept eagerly back to the room where everyone was sleeping.

Zack scuttled over to the tiger skeleton and disappeared. Toby,

Bart, Azzan and Jelly scrambled up the wall and hung from the beams right above the sabre-tooth. Max and Ben got into their sleeping bags and lay down in the darkened room. Then Max gave the thumbs-up sign for the fun to begin.

"**Roaaarrrrr!**" Toby, Bart, Azzan and Jelly made loud growling sounds that echoed around the room.

"The gargoylz are doing a great job!" whispered Ben. "That's really realistic."

"**ROAAARRRRR!**" The noise was even louder this time. Kids started stirring.

Lucinda sat bolt upright and looked around. She prodded Poppy and Tiffany awake. "Did you hear that?" she demanded. "Something's growling."

"I bet it's Max and Ben," said Poppy. "They don't scare us!"

"Lucinda . . ." quavered Tiffany. She pointed a shaking finger above her friend's head. "Look."

Lucinda looked. The snarling skull of the sabre-toothed tiger was slowly turning to stare down at her from its empty eye-sockets, its bones clattering. She gawped in horror, opening and closing her mouth like a goldfish.

Ben and Max stuffed their fists in their mouths to stop themselves from laughing out loud and pretended they were asleep.

Lucinda let out a piercing scream, and
Tiffany and Poppy wailed and clutched
each other.

"Good old Zack," giggled Ben. "No
one would guess there's an invisible
gargoyle moving the sabre-tooth!"

Everyone else started to wake up
and look around in a daze. The tiger
immediately became perfectly still on its
stand.

"What's the matter?" asked Mr Widget.
He tried to get up, got caught in his

sleeping bag and fell flat on his face with a crash that made the girls scream again.

"The t–t–tiger's alive!" Poppy managed to gasp. "It's going to eat us."

The girls around Lucinda, Poppy and Tiffany began to whimper. Mrs Stearn turned on the lights and Miss Bleet ran around like a demented sheep, trying to comfort everyone.

"What's going on?" asked Max sleepily, rubbing his eyes.

"Some of us are trying to sleep," moaned Ben.

"Don't worry, boys," quavered Miss Bleet. "The girls had a nightmare, that's all."

"We were awake!" said Lucinda crossly. "The bones moved all by themselves."

"That sabre-tooth's going to maul us if we stay here," cried Tiffany.

"There'll be nothing left except our socks and clipboards!" whimpered Poppy.

"It's not alive," said Miss Bleet, looking anxiously over her shoulder at the sabre-toothed tiger.

"Of course not," said Max. "I know a bit about sabre-toothed tiger skeletons, and you'd definitely hear it roaring before it came to bite your head off."

Lucinda and her friends shrieked and ran off to huddle between Mrs Stearn and Miss Bleet. The teachers settled them down again, away from the skeleton, and eventually everyone dropped off to sleep, even the three terrified girls.

Max and Ben dragged their sleeping bags right under the sabre-tooth.

"A perfect spot for a good night's sleep!" whispered Ben. "Come on out, gargoylz – it's safe now."

Pop! Zack appeared out of thin air.

"Teeth and bones!" he chanted in their ears. "Teeth and bones!"

The rest of the gargoylz scampered over.

"Good work," whispered Max. "That was a fantastic prank."

"Spluttering gutterz!" declared Toby. "I haven't had so much fun since I trotted round the church under a fruit bowl and the vicar thought I was a giant tortoise."

"Did you enjoy yourself, Jelly?" asked Max.

"It was jolly good fun," said the little pterodactyl happily. Then he opened his beak in a huge yawn. "I've missed playing tricks. But I'm ever so tired now."

Bart pulled open Max's sleeping bag. "Come on then," he said, making room for Jelly. "We'll all get some sleep."

"Ready for more pranks tomorrow," said Azzan cheerfully, climbing in with Ben, Toby and Zack.

"I can't wait," said Ben with a grin.

3. Jelly's Jolly Joke

The next morning Max and Ben hurried
the gargoylz off to the storeroom before
anyone else woke up.

"We're going home after breakfast,"
Ben explained to Toby, Bart, Zack and
Azzan. "So you'd better get yourselves into
our cases before the others wake up."

"It was nice to meet you, Jelly,"
said Max, bending down to the little
pterodactyl, whose beak was drooping
sadly. "I'm sorry we can't stay longer. We'll
come and visit you as soon as we can."

When everyone was dressed and

packed, Alison gave them all a voucher.

"You can have anything you want for breakfast at the café," she told them.

The hungry classmates set off like a herd of rampaging rhinos to get their meals.

"What a waste of a voucher," said Ben scornfully as everyone else chose toast and cereal. "We could eat that boring food at home."

"I'm going to have volcanic bangers and mash!" declared Max, eyeing up the mountain of fluffy mashed potatoes with sausages bursting from the top.

"Dinoburger and cookies for me, please!" Ben said to the man serving the breakfasts.

"That's going to taste a bit funny," said Max.

"The cookies are for the gargoylz," Ben whispered. "We'll stuff them in our pockets as soon as we sit down." He gave his best wide-eyed smile – and the man slopped two extra spoonfuls of relish on his giant burger.

Breakfast over, the boys headed the rush for the gift shop.

"I'm getting some dinosaur poo chocolate for my annoying little sister,"

Max told Ben. "Mum told me to get her something."

"I don't know what I'm going to buy," said Ben. He looked around the shop and his eyes lit up. "Perfect!" he declared. "A model pterodactyl to remind us of Jelly." Then his face fell. "It's too expensive. I'll have to find something else."

He was soon back, waving a postcard of a ferocious sabre-toothed tiger prowling along through prehistoric trees. "We'll give this to Theo when we get back," he told Max. "He'll be really pleased."

Theo's special power was turning into a fierce tiger. At least, he *thought* he turned into a fierce tiger, but as he was a very young gargoyle – only four hundred and twelve years old – he could only manage a cute stripy kitten.

"Brilliant plan, Agent Neal," said Max. "Now, back to the sleepover room. There's loads of facts about sabre-tooths on the sign by the skeleton. We'll write them down, then we can tell Theo about it when we get home."

Miss Bleet was flapping around like an anxious mother hen as she tried to round up her class, ready for the journey home.

"Good gracious!" she exclaimed weakly as she saw Max and Ben earnestly writing sabre-tooth facts on their clipboards.

"Are you all right, miss?" asked Ben.

"Oh yes, yes," croaked Miss Bleet, clutching a nearby pillar for support. "I was just a little surprised to see you working. Home time now."

"Teachers!" Ben whispered to Max when she'd tottered off. "They can't cope with sleepovers."

Max nodded sympathetically and shoved the notes into his rucksack. "It looks like everyone's ready to go," he told Ben. "We'd better get our cases. I hope the gargoylz are safely inside."

They pushed open the door of the storeroom. Their bags were the only two left in there, and the boys could see the sides bulging with bumpy gargoyle shapes.

Ben grinned. "They're ready."

"Goodbye, Jelly, wherever you are," called Max.

There was no reply.

"He must be frozen somewhere in

here," said Ben. "He can't risk anyone seeing him." He slipped his postcard into a pocket of his suitcase and hauled the case along. "Wow!" he said in amazement. "This feels a lot heavier than it did when we arrived. That postcard must weigh more than I thought."

The class was soon crammed into an Underground train. Ben looked down to check his case and saw Bart eyeing him through the tiny gap in the zip.

"You've got your knee in my belly," Bart complained.

"Sorry," said Ben, trying to move.

"I've got lots of room," Toby called cheerfully from Max's case, "now that Azzan's got out."

"Got out?" gasped Max. "Where is he?"

"Where's who?" asked Miss Bleet. "Who's missing?"

"No one," said Max quickly.

The boys scanned the crowded carriage as Miss Bleet frantically started counting heads.

"There he is!" whispered Ben. He pointed to a woman in a large fluffy anorak who was standing nearby. Azzan was fast asleep inside her hood.

"How are we going to get him out?" hissed Ben.

74

"Leave this to me, Agent Neal," muttered Max. "Excuse me, madam," he said loudly. "I think you've dropped something."

As the woman bent forward to look, Max snatched Azzan and shoved him inside his coat.

"Good work, Agent Black!" exclaimed Ben.

But Max had gone bright red in the face and was hopping from foot to foot.

"Keep still!" whispered Ben. "Mrs Stearn's looking."

"I can't help it," groaned Max. "Azzan keeps snorting fire." He stuck his head in his coat. "Behave yourself in there!" he called.

"I'm not doing anything," said an old woman indignantly.

At that moment the train drew into a station. "Everyone out!" called Mr Widget.

"A lucky escape!" exclaimed Max, diving for the door.

As soon as they were on the overground train home, Max and Ben headed for the best window seats, making sure no one else could squeeze in with them. They put their cases up against the glass and their rucksacks on the table between them. There were luggage racks on the other side of the carriage so no one else could see what they were up to.

The four gargoylz immediately scrambled out. The boys gave them a handful of cookies and they munched away happily.

"Dangling drainpipes, that was a great trip!" said Toby. "I haven't had so much fun since we put squashed raisinz in the vicar's sandwich and he thought he was eating beetlz."

"I love sleepoverz! I love sleepoverz!" chanted Zack, dancing on the table.

"How about you, Bart?" asked Ben. "We were a bit worried you weren't going to enjoy yourself."

"Whatever gave you that idea?" said the tubby little gargoyle, a beaming smile on his face. "I love museumz. In fact I've got a museum joke. What do you call a sleeping triceratops? A dino-snore!"

The gargoylz rolled about on the seats holding their sides.

"I've got another one! Why can't you hear a pterodactyl go to the toilet?" spluttered Bart.

"I don't know," chanted his friends. "Why can't you hear a pterodactyl go to the toilet?"

"Because it has a silent P!" came a chirpy voice. And then, to Max and Ben's astonishment, Ben's case began to wriggle. Then a long stony beak popped out, and then Jelly scrambled out and perched on the seat. "I told Bart that one," he said proudly.

"Jelly!" gasped Max, looking worried. "How did you get in there?"

"I nipped in, just like the otherz," laughed Jelly. He peeped out of the window. "I haven't seen the world for a long, long time. Trainz go a jolly sight faster than they used to."

"I invited Jelly to come home with us," said Bart nervously. He gave an embarrassed burp and a tiny spider popped out of his mouth and scuttled off. "He was lonely in the museum so I told him he'd find lots of new friendz if he came to live on St Mark's church."

"It was a very kind thought," Ben assured him, "and we'd love it if Jelly came to live with you. But I'm afraid he'll have to go back."

"It's stealing from the museum if we keep him," Max explained.

The gargoylz looked horrified and Jelly began to melt.

"He can't be stolen," insisted Azzan, leaping to Jelly's defence. "He's not a thing or a pet."

"Only thingz and pets can be stolen," added Toby. "Jelly's a gargoyle and he *chose* to come with us."

"He escaped!" put in Bart.

"Maybe," said Ben, "but—"

"He didn't even belong to the museum in the first place," Toby pointed out.

"True," began Max, "but—"

"If anyone tries to take him back I'll singe their bottom!" said Azzan fiercely.

"Burned bum!" chanted Zack. "Burned bum!"

"And anyway," Jelly piped up, "the

museum people have forgotten I exist. I've always stayed hidden."

The gargoylz looked pleadingly at the boys.

"So no one will miss you at the museum?" said Max.

"No one," declared the little pterodactyl.

"And we're not stealing you?" added Ben.

Jelly shook his head.

Big grins spread slowly over Max and Ben's faces. "Then you can come!" they said together.

The gargoylz gave a huge cheer.

"What's all this noise?" came a weedy voice.

Max's spy radar leaped into life: short and dumpy, limp brown hair, face like a scared rabbit. He knew what that meant. It was Enemy Agent Miss Bleet, codename: Wimpy Teacher.

The gargoylz shot back into the cases as Miss Bleet lurched into view, gripping the seats tightly to keep her balance.

"Max and I were just practising our sabre-toothed tiger roar," Ben told her. "It's very realistic, isn't it, miss?"

"Oh . . . yes indeed," stammered Miss Bleet. "I'm glad to see that you boys have got so much out of your trip."

"Oh, yes, you can't *imagine* how much we've got out of it!" said Max, glancing at the Jelly-shaped bulge in Ben's suitcase.

Ben snorted with laughter and tried to turn it into a cough. It came out as a sort of trumpeting sound. "That was my woolly mammoth," he explained.

"No more prehistoric animal sounds now," said Miss Bleet wearily. "We're coming to Oldacre Station and we don't want to scare the ticket collector."

As soon as their class reached the school playground, Max and Ben sneaked

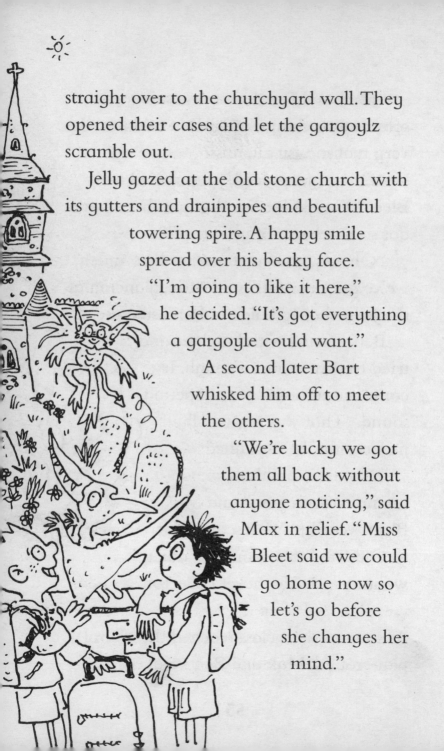

straight over to the churchyard wall. They opened their cases and let the gargoylz scramble out.

Jelly gazed at the old stone church with its gutters and drainpipes and beautiful towering spire. A happy smile spread over his beaky face. "I'm going to like it here," he decided. "It's got everything a gargoyle could want."

A second later Bart whisked him off to meet the others.

"We're lucky we got them all back without anyone noticing," said Max in relief. "Miss Bleet said we could go home now so let's go before she changes her mind."

"First we'd better do some superspy work and sneak into school," said Ben. "We need to collect the things we left behind. My mum will go mad if I get home without my sleepover stuff."

"Outrageous!" came a familiar voice. It was Mrs Hogsbottom. The evil head teacher seemed to be weighed down under a mountain of pyjamas, toothbrushes and underpants. The boys suddenly realized it was *their* pyjamas, toothbrushes and underpants.

"Max Black and Ben Neal," thundered the scary head teacher. "You have broken school rule number six hundred and fifty-three – boys must not hide essential night-time equipment under their desks and then go running off on school trips." She fixed her beady eyes on them. "I have written a list of all the school rules you two have broken and I have run out of paper. School rule number seven hundred and nineteen states that boys must not make their head teacher run out of paper! I am very—"

Splat! A squishy purple ball hit her on the back of the head. The pants and pyjamas flew up into the air as Mrs Hogsbottom spun round to see who'd thrown it.

"That jelly ball looks familiar, Agent Neal," whispered Max.

"It *is* very gloopy, Agent Black," agreed Ben.

The boys looked up at the church. A row of gargoyle eyes gleamed mischievously back at them.

"Jelly!" Max and Ben exclaimed together.

The ball, having rebounded off the head teacher's bun, was now bouncing across the playground. It rolled to a stop

at Barry Price's feet. Barry,
the school bully, also known
as The Basher, was busy
pinching a Frisbee from one
of the infants. But as soon
as he saw the jelly ball, he
dropped the Frisbee and
picked it up with an
evil grin.

"Outrageous!"
screeched Mrs Hogsbottom, storming over
to him.

"The Basher's in trouble now," muttered
Ben in delight.

"And Mrs Hogsbum's forgotten all
about us!" added Max happily.

The Basher took one look at the
charging head teacher and dropped the
jelly ball as if it was red-hot. The ball
bounced across to the churchyard wall
and turned back into Jelly.

"Did you like my prank?" he asked,

shaking the playground grit off his back. "I did it all on my own."

"It was awesome!" said Max.

"Thanks, Jelly," added Ben, as he and Max picked up their stuff and rammed it into their cases. "You saved us from a big telling off."

"It was jolly good fun!" said the little stony pterodactyl. He waved at the other gargoylz, who gave him the thumbs – and claws – up. "I'm off to tell Bart all about it." And with that, he jumped over the wall, scrambled up a drainpipe and disappeared across the church roof.

"Turns out we didn't need to buy that expensive pterodactyl model in the shop, Agent Neal," said Max as they waved him off.

"You're right, Agent Black," said Ben with a huge grin. "Jelly's the real thing!"

4. Theo-the-sabre-toothed-tiger

It was the morning after the school trip and Max and Ben were sitting in their classroom waiting for the first lesson to start.

"Settle down, class," said Miss Bleet, who was standing by the whiteboard.

Gradually everyone stopped talking.

"We're going to work on a project today," their teacher announced.

Max slumped on his desk. "That's unfair, miss. We're tired out from our trip," he protested.

"You can work in twos," Miss Bleet

went on, ignoring him, "and write about something you saw at the museum."

"That's different!" exclaimed Ben eagerly. "Why didn't you say so in the first place? We saw loads of cool stuff on our trip."

He and Max got into a secret huddle.

"The best thing was the sabre-toothed tiger," said Max.

SECRET CODEWORD: FUN

"Then that's our project," Ben decided. He fished out the postcard they'd bought for Theo. "We took loads of notes. We'll call our project 'Fang-tastic Facts'."

"And if you draw pictures yourselves," came Miss Bleet's voice, "you'll be excused homework for the rest of the week."

The class cheered.

"There's just one problem, Agent Black," whispered Ben. "We're not very good at drawing."

Max sat bolt upright. "I've had a brilliant idea, Agent Neal," he whispered back. "We could ask Theo to model for us. He can put rulers in his mouth for fangs."

"I bet he'd love to help," said Ben. "He thinks he's a fierce tiger already."

"We'll ask him at playtime when we give him his postcard," said Max. "This is going to be the best project in the history of best projects."

The moment the bell rang, the boys ran out into the playground, dashing over to the church wall.

"Gargoylz!" called Max.

There was no reply.

"That's odd," said Ben. "I can't see a sign of a wing or a whisker." He peered up at the church. "No, wait a minute — there's Toby and Ira and Bart, high up on the roof."

He waved madly at them but the three gargoylz didn't even twitch. They hung upside-down from the gutters in ugly, frozen poses.

"Weird!" said Max, shading his eyes. "Azzan's on the spire but he's turned into a statue as well."

He put his fingers to his mouth and gave a whistle. The gargoylz didn't move.

"We'll have to come back later," said Ben, disappointed, "and find out what's wrong."

"Two missions for lunch time, Agent Neal," muttered Max. "Number one – check on gargoylz. Number two – find Theo for our drawings."

After the longest maths lesson in the world, it was lunch time at last.

The boys bolted down their fishcakes and fries and got to the church wall in record time.

"It looks like the gargoylz haven't moved at all," said Max, feeling puzzled.

"Coo-ee!" came a whisper from the long grass in the churchyard. The boys looked down to see a stripy whiskered face peering up at them.

"Wotcha, Theo!" exclaimed Ben in delight. "What's happened to the others? They're all frozen."

"It's the vicar," Theo told them, glancing round nervously. "He keeps dashing out with a telescope to stare at the roof."

"Why?" asked Max.

"He's gabbling on about spotting a new gargoyle," said Theo.

"Uh-oh!" said Ben. "He's seen Jelly, hasn't he?"

Theo nodded. "So we've not had a minute's peace. Every time we think about coming down to play, he bursts out of the church door to stare at us. I only just managed to hide behind this gravestone before he saw me out of position."

"Well, we're glad you're here," said Max, "because we've got you a present from the museum." He pulled out the postcard. "Look, it's a picture of a sabre-toothed tiger."

Theo sprang up to sit beside them on the wall and took the postcard in his paws, looking at it in delight. "It's a portrait of one of my ancestorz. Jelly told me all about the huge skeleton at the museum."

"We're doing a project on sabre-tooths," said Ben, "and we need your help."

"Of course," said Theo. "If you need help with tigerz then I'm your gargoyle." He stiffened suddenly, his ears twitching. "Dangling drainpipes! The vicar's coming." He jumped down from the wall and dived behind another gravestone.

"He goes to his line-dancing class this afternoon," Theo whispered urgently to the boys. "Come back after school."

"You're on," said Max.

★ ★ ★

The moment the bell rang for the end of school, Max and Ben raced off down the corridor, carrying pages of sabre-tooth facts that they'd spent all afternoon copying out in their best handwriting.

They made a quick stop to ring their mums and tell them they'd be late. Then they were off to the churchyard.

"Mum was very impressed that I wanted to stay behind for a project," said Max.

"So was mine," said Ben. "In fact she was gobsmacked. I don't know why."

"Greetingz!" came a growly purr from a nearby headstone.

Max's spy radar leaped into action: monkey face, big pointy ears, cheeky grin. He knew what that meant. It was Toby, codename: Gargoyle Friend. The little gargoyle flew up and perched on Max's shoulder.

Four pairs of stony eyes peeped round the headstone.

"The vicar's gone at last," said Bart, plodding out. Theo, Azzan and Ira were close behind.

"He's a pesky landlubber!" squawked Ira, flapping his wings. Ira looked like a sort of parroty eagle, and behaved like a pirate.

"Where's Jelly?" asked Max.

"Here I am," said the little pterodactyl, jumping down from the roof. "I was just dusting off my new perch under a turret."

"Have you settled in?" asked Ben.

"Yes, thank you," declared Jelly. "It's whizzo here! Any tricks planned for today?"

"The boyz have got a project," Azzan told him eagerly. "And they need Theo to help."

Pop! Zack appeared in the middle of them. "School work?" he said in surprise. "Can't we do pranks instead?"

"We've got to do school work," said Max as he and Ben sat down on the grass.

"But this school work is fun," said Ben. "We've already got loads of fang-tastic facts." He waved their project pages at the gargoylz.

"Sabre-toothed tigers were as big as lions and as heavy as grizzly bears," Max told them.

"And their fangs were awesome!" added Ben.

Toby peered at their work. "Looks like you've finished your project," he said admiringly. "You should get top marks."

"But we have to add pictures," Max explained, "and we've got to draw them ourselves."

Ben turned to Theo. "Would you be our model?" he asked.

Theo puffed himself up importantly. "I'd be delighted," he said. "It will be easy for me to look like one of my fierce ancestorz with my special tiger power." He wriggled his bottom, turned into a fluffy kitten and gave a growly miaow. "Hope I'm not too scary."

"We'll try and be brave," Max assured him.

"There's one thing missing," said Ben, pulling two short rulers out of his rucksack. "You need longer fangs."

Theo put the rulers in his mouth so
they hung down like long teeth. He tried
to roar and they fell out with a clatter.

"We need something to stick them
in with," said Max. He took a piece of
bubble gum out of his pocket. "This should
do."

He rolled the gum into two balls, stuck
them on the rulers and fixed them onto
Theo's teeth.

"Great!" said Ben. "Now do a scary
pose."

Theo-the-sabre-toothed-tiger arched
his back and tried to look fierce.

"Well done, Theo," Max
said, although Theo
actually looked
rather sweet.

"That's perfect,"
added Ben.

The boys
began drawing.

"Now pretend you're pouncing on a woolly mammoth," suggested Max.

Theo-the-sabre-toothed-tiger stood on his back legs and batted the air. He looked as if he was playing with a ball of string.

Azzan leaned over Ben's shoulder, his hot breath warming Ben's ear. "Give him big pawz," he said.

"And a long tail," added Bart, nudging Ben's elbow.

Ira popped up from under the drawing. "Make him as scary as a sea monster!" he squawked.

Zack, Jelly and Toby crowded round Max.

"Put sharp points on his teeth," demanded Toby.

"Long fangz!" shrieked Zack. "Long fangz!" He jiggled Max so hard that the pencil was nearly pushed across the picture.

"Stop jostling," said Max.

"But we want to join in," said Jelly. "It looks like jolly good fun."

"Here you are. You can draw some pictures of your own," said Ben, handing out paper while Max gave out the coloured pencils.

The boys and the gargoylz scribbled away until there was a huge pile of drawings on the path.

"You've been a great model, Theo,"

said Max at last, sitting back on his heels to admire his drawing of a sabre-toothed tiger leaping over a waterfall.

"Yes, thanks, Theo," added Ben, colouring in some purple prehistoric mountains behind his fierce beast. "We couldn't have done it without you."

They jumped as the church clock struck five.

"We've got to go," gasped Max.

Ben started to gather up all the drawings. "We mustn't be late for tea," he said. "But the project and pictures have got to be put together."

"Leave it all with us," said Toby. "We'll pick up the pictures. There's plenty of time before the vicar gets back."

"But it's got to be ready to hand in tomorrow," said Max, shoving his pencils in his rucksack.

"Don't worry," insisted Bart. "We'll have it all neat and tidy and on Miss Bleet's desk first thing tomorrow morning."

"Thanks, gargoylz," chorused the boys as they sped off down the churchyard path.

★ ★ ★

After lunch the next day Max and Ben zoomed into the classroom. They were looking forward to getting their project back. Miss Bleet had already congratulated them for having it on her table so early that morning. She had no idea that it had actually arrived before they had, thanks to the invisible Zack!

"Well done, Lucinda and Tiffany," she said, holding out a pink file. "That was a lovely project on prehistoric ponies."

"Boring!" whispered Max.

She carried on handing out work. At last it was the boys' turn. She picked up the pieces of paper, which had all been tied together with one of the vicar's shoelaces.

"Max and Ben," she said. "I'm very pleased with your hard work." She began to leaf through the pages. "But I'm puzzled by some of your pictures. For example, I'm not sure that sabre-toothed tigers breathed fire."

She held up a drawing the boys hadn't seen before. Theo-the-sabre-toothed-tiger was on a grassy plain, flames shooting out of his mouth. The class gasped in amazement.

"Azzan must have done that one!" Max whispered to Ben. "The gargoylz have handed in all *their* pictures as well as ours!"

"Ah, but how do you know sabre-tooths *didn't* breathe fire, miss?" said Ben quickly. "And if they did, we had to have a picture of it."

"I suppose anything's possible," twittered Miss Bleet. "What about this one?"

She showed the class a picture of Theo-the-sabre-toothed-tiger guzzling a plate of freshly baked cookies. The class started to giggle.

"Er . . ." said Max, thinking quickly. "Sabre-tooths can't have only eaten meat. That would have been boring, so we thought they would have eaten cookies too."

"They probably stole them from the woolly mammoths," finished Ben.

"Good answer, Agent Neal," whispered Max. "Luckily she hasn't noticed that that picture's signed Toby!"

"Well . . . all right," said their teacher, shuffling through the pile. "But I'm really not sure about this one!"

The whole class laughed and clapped, and Max and Ben gawped at the page.

Miss Bleet was holding up a brightly

coloured picture of Theo-the-sabre-toothed-tiger walking the plank of a pirate ship.

"That must have been Ira's!" whispered Max.

"Well, er, we did that one for you, miss," said Ben in a rush. "It's modern art."

Miss Bleet went pink and beamed. "Oh! Thank you, boys," she said, sticking the picture proudly on the wall. "You've all done very well, class. No homework for the rest of the week. And you can have an extra ten minutes' playtime now."

She stood and stared happily at Ira's picture as they all ran outside.

Max and Ben made straight for the churchyard wall.

Bart came scuttling out from behind a

bush. He put his fingers in
his mouth and whistled.
Toby, Theo, Azzan,
Ira, Zack and Jelly
popped up from the
long grass.

"We've been
waiting for you,"
said Toby eagerly.
"Did Miss Bleet like
our project?"

"She did," Max told the
gargoylz, grinning. "Especially
your pictures."

"The whole class liked them," added
Ben. "Thanks, gargoylz."

The gargoylz grinned happily.

"We haven't had so much fun since we dropped a red pen into the vicar's washing machine and dyed all his socks pink," said Toby with a chuckle.

"I've got a picture for you, boyz," said Jelly. "And it's jolly good, if I do say so myself." He carefully unfolded a colourful drawing and handed it to them. A sabre-

toothed tiger was bounding along, with Max and Ben riding proudly on its back.

"That's me," said Theo. "Don't I look fierce?"

"*Very* fierce. It's awesome!" gasped Ben.

"Thank you, Jelly," exclaimed Max. "It's fang-tastic!"

Gargoylz Fact File

Full name: Tobias the Third
Known as: Toby
Special Power: Flying
Likes: All kinds of pranks and mischief – especially playing jokes on the vicar
Dislikes: Mrs Hogsbottom, garden gnomes

Full name: Barnabas
Known as: Barney
Special Power: Making big stinks!
Likes: Cookiez
Dislikes: Being surprised by humanz

Name: Eli
Special Power: Turning into a grass snake
Likes: Sssports Day, Sssslithering
Dislikes: Ssscary ssstories

Full name: Bartholomew
Known as: Bart
Special Power: Burping spiders

Likes: Being grumpy

Dislikes: Being told to cheer up

Full name: Theophilus
Known as: Theo
Special Power: Turning into a ferocious tiger (well, tabby kitten!)

Likes: Sunny spots and cosy places

Dislikes: Rain

Full name: Zackary
Known as: Zack
Special Power: Making himself invisible to humanz

Likes: Bouncing around, eating bramblz, thistlz, and anything with Pricklz!

Dislikes: Keeping still

Name: Azzan
Special Power: Breathing fire

Likes: Surprises

Dislikes: Smoke going up his nose and making him sneeze

Full name: Jehieli

Known as: Jelly

Special Power: Turning to jelly

Likes: Having friendz to play with

Dislikes: Bulliez and spoilsports

Name: Ira

Special Power: Making it rain

Likes: Making humanz walk the plank

Dislikes: Being bored

Name: Cyrus

Special Power: Singing lullabies to send humanz to sleep

Likes: Fun dayz out

Dislikes: Snoring

Name: Rufus

Special Power: Turning into a skeleton

Likes: Playing spooky tricks

Dislikes: Squeezing into small spaces